CRASHING
THE PARTY

BY PERDITA FINN

SCHOLASTIC INC.
New York   Toronto   London   Auckland   Sydney
Mexico City   New Delhi   Hong Kong   Buenos Aires

For Dante and Balthazar,

the original Time Flyers

ISBN-13: 978-0-439-74436-2
ISBN-10: 0-439-74436-9

Text copyright © 2007 by Perdita Finn
Illustrations copyright © 2007 by Scholastic Inc.

12 11 10 9 8 7 6 5 4 3 2 1   7 8 9 10 11 12/0

Printed in the U.S.A.
First printing, January 2007

Cover and chapter opener illustrations by Brandon Dorman
Additional illustrations by Mike Moran

1 BE MY GUEST

Katie was just about to order a hot fudge sundae when she saw it out the window of the restaurant. A sudden bolt of blue light flashed through the falling snow. Her older brother, Josh, saw it, too, and then just at that moment, they both heard it — an enormous sonic boom. The two children looked at each other. No question about it — another Time Flyer had just arrived.

"That's strange," said Mrs. Lexington, putting down her coffee cup. "You don't usually get thunder and lightning at this time of year."

"Jets," said Mr. Lexington, knowingly. "New top secret jets. Bet that's what it was."

"We've got to go," said Katie.

"Yup, gotta go," agreed her brother.

"But, kids," said their father. "We haven't even ordered dessert."

"And I haven't finished my coffee," said Mrs. Lexington. "There's no hurry. I haven't had a chance to do any grocery shopping, and I know the two of you will be saying you're hungry before we walk in the door. Why don't you get that sundae, Katie? I'll just have one bite of it."

Katie bit her lip, unsure of what to say. There was a lot she and her brother knew about the Time Flyers student exchange program that their parents didn't. Like the fact that the kids didn't just come from other countries but from back in time as well. "Mom, didn't you say we'd be getting another Time Flyer before the holidays?"

"I think so, sweetie, but I haven't heard a word from the director, Mr. Dee."

"That's not unusual," said Mr. Lexington. "Worst run program I've ever seen. Kids arriving in the middle of the night with no luggage and no toothpaste. . . ."

"I think another one might already be at home," said Josh urgently. "Just a hunch." He didn't like to think about what might happen if some prehistoric kid was left alone for too long in their twenty-first-century ranch house. There had been bathroom problems in the past.

"All right, all right," said their father. "Give me a minute to pay the bill."

On the drive home Josh and Katie barely listened to their mother as she pointed out holiday decorations in the neighborhood. "Ooh, look at that house! I just love that light-up Santa!"

"Usual routine, right?" Josh whispered to his sister in the backseat.

"Yup. Find the kid, go over electric lights, cars, blue jeans . . ."

"And bathrooms," interrupted her brother.

"And bathrooms." Katie sighed. "Honestly, I'm not sure I'm up to another one."

"Me, either," said Josh.

The car pulled into the driveway. As the Lexingtons stepped onto the walkway, the outdoor lights clicked on, revealing enormous trunks and wooden boxes strewn across the front lawn, their tops lightly covered in snowflakes.

"Getting a jump on the Christmas shopping, honey?" asked Mr. Lexington, confused.

"What can all this possibly be?" said Mrs. Lexington, opening a hatbox and pulling out what looked like a blue velvet pancake covered in enormous feathers.

"I don't think our new Time Flyer travels light," commented Josh.

Just at that moment the front door opened, and standing in the glow of the porch lamp was a girl who looked about Josh's age. She was wearing a yellow silk dress with so many flounces, ribbons, and laces that she looked like a wedding cake. It was so wide that the girl couldn't even fit through the door and had to come out to the porch sideways. Strangely, her hair was completely white and piled in curls at least a foot high on top of her head.

"It's a Christmas angel," exclaimed Mr. Lexington.

"*Charmant! Charmant!*" The girl laughed, her voice as light as a silver bell. "But I am only Adèle Hélene Marie Louise Marguerite de la Bouche, the eldest daughter and only child of the Marquise de la Bouche. You must be Monsieur Lexington."

"You're from France, aren't you?" asked Mr. Lexington.

"*Oui*, monsieur!" She waved a fan in front of her face and laughed again.

Mr. Lexington beamed. "Hear that, kids? That's what French sounds like!"

"You may carry in my things, monsieur, and place them in my room, *s'il vous plaît*." She smiled prettily at Mr. Lexington.

"Why, I'd be honored, young lady," he said, blushing.

"Honored?" Josh whispered to Katie.

"I wish he'd be 'honored' to carry my backpack sometimes," said Katie.

"And, Madame Lexington," continued the girl in a sharper tone, pointing her fan at a wooden case Mrs. Lexington was examining. "Do be careful with that one. It holds the eight strings of diamonds the queen lent me for my visit." The girl made a graceful turn, then glided back into the house. As she did so, a fine mist of white powder fell from her hair and mixed with the new snow on the porch.

"Guess you kids were right." Mrs. Lexington shook her head. "Glad I didn't remove the air mattress from your room, Katie."

"Aren't we lucky," said Mr. Lexington. "A visitor from France. Now that's class!"

"Here, Dad," said Josh. "Help me with one of these trunks."

"Whoa!" said Mr. Lexington as he bent down to pick one up. "What's she got in here? Cannonballs?"

"Let's hope not," said Katie under her breath. She had learned to be ready for anything when a Time Flyer arrived.

When the family trudged inside, each carrying a box or a trunk, they saw Adèle Hélene Marie Louise Marguerite de la Bouche already lounging on the couch. "Thank you. Thank you," she

6

gushed without moving a muscle. "You *are* good people. Le Comte du Dee assured me I would find you most entertaining. Now, madam," she said, directing her attention to Mrs. Lexington, who was still trying to catch her breath after just putting down an enormous box. "Let the others concern themselves with my things, *s'il vous plaît*, and look to my supper." She smiled prettily and batted her eyelashes. "Mama usually sends our own chef ahead to the inn to prepare our food to our liking, but Le Comte du Dee explained to me that would be quite impossible on this little adventure. Oh, I am so thrilled to be here! Life at court can be so dull, you know." She lay back on the cushions of the couch and sighed dramatically.

Josh and Katie stared at each other. They'd hosted a kid who didn't know how to bathe, a boy who didn't wear clothes, and a stuck-up Puritan who actually liked to do chores, but at that moment they knew they were in for their biggest challenge yet.

"So, how long are you staying, anyway?" Katie blurted out. She peered at the golden hourglass that hung from the girl's neck. All Time Flyers carried an hourglass that allowed them to be transported through time. How quickly the sand poured through it indicated how long the Time Flyer would be staying.

"Yes, dear," seconded a somewhat flustered Mrs. Lexington. "Will you be with us for the holidays?"

"Ah! I regret that I will not! I must return for the balls. I am all the rage, you see, and the queen will miss me if I am not there. I am here for only a week."

"Hear that, kids? She's got to get back to see the queen. I could tell we were in for a treat the moment I saw her," gushed Mr. Lexington, beaming. "Betsy, you should get our new guest something to eat."

Mrs. Lexington gave her husband an anxious look. "Abner, I don't know that I have anything. That's why we went out to eat. . . ."

"C'mon, Dad," said Josh, straining to hold up his end of the trunk. "Let's get this luggage upstairs. And, Katie, why don't you get to know our guest?"

"Good idea," answered Katie. She needed a moment alone with the new Time Flyer to clue her in fast.

Mrs. Lexington headed toward the kitchen, and the new girl immediately sat up and called after her, "Do not go to too much trouble, madam. Some soup and a little pâté, a veal roast with sorrel, a boiled pigeon, a custard tart, and perhaps some fruit and whipped cream."

Mrs. Lexington tried to smile. "You know, we weren't expecting you, dear, and I just haven't gotten to the grocery store. I don't even think I have a can of soup. How about a sandwich?"

"Betsy makes a great PB and J, Adèle," Mr. Lexington called down from upstairs.

"P, B, and J?" The girl looked dumbfounded.

"Or how about a bowl of cereal?" said Mrs. Lexington, brightly.

"Oh, la . . ." said the girl, pouting. "I had so hoped for a capon. . . . I suppose a cup of chocolate will have to do." She sighed again. "Le comte did tell me I would face challenges on this trip, and I am very brave, you know. Everyone says so."

"I'm sure you are, dear," said Mrs. Lexington with a forced smile. "One cup of cocoa coming up."

"So, what do they call you for short?" asked Katie as soon as her mother was out of the room.

"Pardon?" The girl didn't even bother to look at Katie when she said it.

"Your name. Mine's Katie. What's yours?"

"Adèle Hélene Marie Louise Marguerite —"

"I'm calling you Adèle Hélene. Okay?"

"I would prefer Mademoiselle de la Bouche. After all, my family does go back to the fourteenth century, and I am quite sure that yours does not."

"While you're here in the twenty-first century, you are Adèle Hélene. By the way, you do know you are in the twenty-first century in America?"

"Yes. Yes," said Adèle Hélene with irritation. "Le comte explained it all. Just as the queen plays at being a peasant at Trianon, I will experience the life of a bourgeois in the future. I suppose it should all be very exciting, but I am at this moment finding myself quite fatigued. I think I shall call you *Rien. Le Petit Rien.*"

"What's that mean?"

"Oh, nothing." Adèle Hélene laughed in a way Katie didn't like.

"You're from France?" Katie said. "But what year are you from?"

"Seventeen eighty-eight, and yes, yes, I know I am hundreds of years in the future and there are all kinds of inventions that will astound and amaze me. Thus far, however, I am not impressed."

"Seventeen eighty-eight?" questioned Katie, something nagging at the back of her mind. "Is that before or after the Revolution?"

"Ah," snorted Adèle Hélene, disgusted. "Not to know when your own country fought for its freedom. After. After, *Petit Rien.* My father, you know, was the head of a battalion in America. You never would have defeated the British without us." She tapped her fan against her dress.

"Right," said Katie distractedly. Something was bothering her. Something she would have to look into later.

"Did I hear you say your father has been to America?" said Mr. Lexington, coming back into the room with Josh and carrying another trunk.

Adèle Hélene instantly sat up and smiled at Mr. Lexington. "He commanded a regiment!"

Mr. Lexington nodded his head, clearly impressed. "Military man, is he?"

"Nobility, monsieur, nobility," corrected Adèle Hélene. "May I give you a little nickname, monsieur? A *sobriquet*, we call it. Already I have named your daughter *Le Petit Rien*."

"That sounds adorable," said Mr. Lexington, clearly delighted.

"Maybe," said Katie, uncertain. "She still hasn't told me what it means."

"Oh, but I did." Adèle Hélene laughed. "Now for your sweet father. You will be *Monsieur Poulet*, I think."

"*Monsieur Poulet*," repeated Mr. Lexington. "That sounds pretty fancy!"

At that moment, Mrs. Lexington returned to the living room with a cup of cocoa and a plate of cookies. "Here you go, dear. I hope that will fill you up until I get to the store tomorrow."

Adèle Hélene waved her fan toward the coffee table, indicating that Mrs. Lexington should just set them down. But when she bit daintily into a cookie, she immediately spit it out. "Pah!" she spluttered. "It tastes like wood. I have heard of the peasants eating bread made from ferns but never thought that I, the daughter of the Marquise de la Bouche, would have to consume such food!"

"Be brave," said Katie, raising an eyebrow at Josh, who snickered.

"I've heard they have awfully fancy food in France," explained Mr. Lexington to his wife.

"And awfully fancy people," said Mrs. Lexington out of Adèle Hélene's earshot.

In the meantime, Adèle Hélene tried the cocoa and spit that out, too. "I am to bed," she announced. She flounced toward the stairs in her enormous dress. "Do not awaken me in the morning. I will arise in time for dinner and you can help me with my hair."

"My couch!" exclaimed Mrs. Lexington looking at where Adèle Hélene had been sitting. All the pillows were encrusted with a sticky white powder from Adèle's hair.

"It's only a week, Betsy." Mr. Lexington patted his wife on the back.

"Just a week," said Mrs. Lexington, looking at her couch.

"A week," echoed Josh.

I hope so, thought Katie. *I really hope so.*

2 CASUAL ATTIRE

"Her Majesty is still snoring away," said Katie when she came downstairs the next morning.

"Now, Katie, be polite to our guest," responded her mother as she put the milk for the cereal on the kitchen table. "This program is all about tolerance, about learning how different people around the world live. That's why I signed up for it in the first place."

"I'm just glad she's not coming to school with us today," said Josh, between gulps of orange juice.

"I'd send her if I could," said Mrs. Lexington. "But can you believe, in all those trunks she doesn't have a single thing to wear? Just all those velvet and silk costumes. Not a single pair of jeans or even a T-shirt. And I'm afraid she's so tiny, she'll never fit into your clothes, Katie. What did she think? That she was coming at Halloween?"

"It's the French, Betsy," said Mr. Lexington, looking up from his morning newspaper. "You've seen those runway models on TV. Look at the outfits they wear. High fashion, they call it. Our new guest is very sophisticated, in case you hadn't noticed."

"That's true, Abner. She does seem like she comes from a very wealthy family. Honestly, I think some of those diamonds she's wearing are real."

At recess that day, Katie stayed in the classroom to do a little research. "When was the French Revolution?" she asked her teacher, Mrs. Chandler.

"Hmmm," said Mrs. Chandler. "Some time after ours, I know, at the end of the eighteenth century."

"That's what I thought," said Katie. "But you don't have an exact date?"

"Why don't you check online?" suggested Mrs. Chandler. "I must say it's nice to see children taking charge of their own education!"

Katie spent the rest of the hour scouring the Internet, and on the way home from school she told Josh what she'd found out. "Her Majesty doesn't know it yet, but if she's really nobility, she and all her friends are just a year or two from losing their heads to the guillotine. She's from seventeen eighty-eight, and things start getting really bad in seventeen eighty-nine."

"Whoa!" said Josh. "Think we should tell her?"

"Probably at some point before she goes back. I mean, everyone who doesn't get out of France starts getting chopped — even the kids."

"Yikes!" said Josh.

No one seemed to be in the house when the two children walked through the door. Mrs. Lexington had been grocery shopping, however, so Katie and Josh put some pizza pockets into the microwave. They were just about to settle down at the kitchen table with their snack to work on their homework, when they heard footsteps on the stairs. Adèle Hélene appeared, yawning, her massive powdered curls all rumpled and squished. She was wearing layers of white lace petticoats, a corset, and a gauzy bathrobe draped around her shoulders. Adèle Hélene slid into a chair and announced with frustration, "I've been waiting and waiting, but no one has brought me a cup of coffee or even any hot water to begin my toilette."

"You're just getting up?" asked Josh.

"*Oui.*"

"Wow," said Katie. "We've already gone to school and come home."

"How sweet, *Petit Rien.*" Adèle Hélene smiled at her.

"That's not my name, Adèle Hélene," insisted Katie.

"Oh, but it is for me! Now you can help me get dressed. I had no idea how I was going to get ready for dinner and the theater without my maid."

"The theater?" said Josh.

"Your maid?" said Katie.

Adèle Hélene stared at them, frowning. "Could

someone please get me a cup of coffee? I am so fatigued."

"Look," said Katie, fuming. "You may not be here for very long, but while you are, we're going to have to get a few things straight. For the next six days, you are in the United States of America and we don't have kings and queens here. And we don't have servants in this family."

"Yes, yes, I know, you silly girl. 'All men are created equal' or whatever it is that Virginia farmer wrote. What do you think I am, an imbecile?"

Katie was just about to answer that question when she heard her mother come in the front door. Mrs. Lexington walked into the kitchen with a shopping bag. "Oh, good, Adèle. You're up. I hated to wake you. I hear that jet lag can be terrible. Now, I've gotten you some clothes. . . ."

"New clothes! Oh, how delicious! I'm glad *someone* knows how to be considerate." She rolled her eyes at Josh and Katie.

"Well, it's nothing too fancy and I was just guessing at sizes." Mrs. Lexington pulled out some clothes from the bag. "I got you a pullover and a hoodie." She held up a blue sweater and sweatshirt. "And two pairs of jeans and, oh, yes, some socks. They were having a great holiday sale at SuperSaver."

Adèle Hélene looked like she was about to throw up. Her mouth turned down and her nose wrinkled. "*C'est horrible!* You cannot expect that I, Adèle Hélene Marie Louise Marguerite de la Bouche, a lady who has been dressed by Rose Bertin herself, could wear these ... these ..." — she gingerly touched the blue jeans — "these coarse peasant rags. The queen wears silk even when she pretends to be a milkmaid. I had no idea what an ordeal this would be!" She covered her face with her hands and began to cry.

Mrs. Lexington took a deep breath and bit her lip.

"It's all about tolerance, Mom," whispered Katie.

"I just want to be fashionable," wept Adèle Hélene. "I just want to look right."

Josh laughed out loud and Adèle Hélene glared at him. "Do you really think it's fashionable to put flour paste in your hair and wear all those frilly clothes?" he asked. "I mean, c'mon. You're in America now." Josh reached over and gave her a friendly pat on the back.

Adèle Hélene looked at him suspiciously. "Do your most acclaimed personages wear such things as these ugly blue pantaloons?"

"Absolutely," said Katie.

"Oh, yes," said Mrs. Lexington. "You know what, dear? I'm going to go get you some magazines and you can see what the girls are wearing in the States. This is what Katie and all her friends like."

For the rest of the afternoon, Adèle Hélene lay on the couch studying Mrs. Lexington's collection of magazines. She tore out pictures, demanded a pen, and circled photos of hairstyles and shoes, then disappeared upstairs while Mrs. Lexington, Katie, and Josh got dinner ready.

"I'm glad the water's running up there," whispered Mrs. Lexington to Katie. "I've heard the French don't bathe as much as we do but, honestly, I think she had bugs in her hair."

"Wouldn't doubt it," said Katie, helping her mother peel carrots for the stew she was making.

The Lexingtons were already sitting at the table when Adèle Hélene finally reappeared. "Voilà," she announced, coming into the room.

Josh dropped his fork. "What a change!"

"Wow!" exclaimed Mr. Lexington. "You look like a movie star."

Adèle Hélene was transformed. Her newly washed hair was shiny and blond and hung straight to her slender waist. She was wearing the jeans, but they were now artfully ripped, with a strand of sapphires elegantly dangling from the side pocket. She'd put on the blue cardigan but peeking through it was a delicately embroidered yellow silk camisole. On her feet were tiny high-heeled satin slippers. It was a winning combination of eighteenth and twenty-first century, with a style that was completely original. She looked amazing.

"What a relief," said Mrs. Lexington. "Now you're all ready to go to school tomorrow with the children."

"School?" said Adèle Hélene. "But I am done with school."

"Not while you're visiting us, you're not," said Mrs. Lexington firmly.

"Mom, if she's done with school, let her stay home," said Katie, imagining what it would be like to have this particular girl in her class.

"I'm sorry, those are the rules of the Time Flyers program, and Adèle Hélene will follow them like everybody else."

"Don't worry," said Mr. Lexington, giving her a wink. "You'll meet a lot of nice kids there. And they'll be impressed with you!"

"But of course they will," said Adèle Hélene. "I always make an impression. It is most agreeable to make an impression."

An impression? thought Katie. That's *exactly* what she didn't want Adèle Hélene to make.

3 INVITATION ONLY

In the car on the way to school, Adèle Hélene yawned and rubbed her eyes and complained about how unpleasant it was to get out of bed so early. She wasn't happy with the car, either. "My father's carriage is pulled by eight horses," she explained to Josh and Katie in the backseat.

"Our car doesn't need any horses," said Josh. "It has horsepower."

Adèle Hélene ignored him and continued. "Our carriage is sky blue and covered in gold."

"Our car is red so my mother can find it in the parking lot," said Katie. And to herself she added, *Please, please don't let her be in my class!*

"Now tell me," Adèle Hélene said, grabbing Katie's arm just before they entered the school. "Who's the rage?"

"Excuse me?" answered Katie.

Adèle Hélene sighed. "The rage. In favor. Don't you Americans understand English?"

Katie jerked herself away. "C'mon, Mom's got to sign you in, and I'm gonna be in a rage if I'm late for class."

As soon as she entered the school, Adèle Hélene suddenly stopped complaining and smiled sweetly at the office ladies. She watched everybody — the cluster of girls chatting on their way to class, the boy who walked in by himself from the bus but was immediately surrounded by a swarm of friends, the teacher making some last-minute copies before class.

And everybody who passed the office noticed her. With her striking hair and elegant clothes, she caught the attention of boys and girls alike. Whenever someone looked at her, her eyes would meet theirs and she would flash one of her winning smiles.

"You'd never know what a boss-machine she is to look at her," Katie whispered to Josh.

"Now, Adèle Hélene," said Mrs. Lexington as she finished Adèle's paperwork. "You'll be in Josh's class with Mrs. Pitney."

"Yes!" said Katie, then quieted when Mrs. Lexington gave her a sharp look.

"Mrs. Pitney will know how to handle Adèle," whispered Josh to Katie about his sixth-grade teacher. "Nobody, and I mean nobody, charms the Pit Bull."

"Just keep her away from Lizzie Markle. You know the routine," responded Katie. Lizzie was the sixth-grade girl who was constantly making trouble for their Time Flyer visitors. She'd nearly gotten the Lexingtons arrested when Humility, a Pilgrim from Plymouth, visited them over Thanksgiving.

"No problem," said Josh, rushing after Adèle Hélene, who had started down the hall without him.

"If you need help with anything, just let me know," he said to Adèle Hélene.

"My dear boy," she said, stopping and looking at him. "Do you think me incapable of handling the social whirl at Alice R. Quigley Middle School? By the way, your shoelace is untied. You know, you really ought to speak to your cobbler. I noticed all the other boys were wearing a much more flattering style."

Josh bent over to fix his shoelace but couldn't figure out what was the matter with the sneakers themselves. By the time he got up, however, Adèle Hélene had vanished into the classroom.

When Josh came in a minute later, the whole class was laughing, even gray-haired, tight-lipped Mrs. Pitney. "Your new guest is so charming, Joshua. How lucky we are to have her here!" She beamed at Adèle Hélene. "She's just been telling us the most amusing story about her convent school in France. Do take a seat, dear. Anywhere you like."

Adèle Hélene pursed her lips and examined the room. "Hmm," she mused. "I wonder . . ."

"Here's an empty seat," blurted out Neil Carmody, Josh's best friend.

"You can sit here," said Talia Fernandez, smiling and pointing at an empty seat beside her.

"Or here," said Suzanne Macintire.

But Adèle Hélene ignored their offers and sauntered over to where Lizzie Markle was doodling in her notebook, exchanging knowing looks with her friends and giggling. "I think I'll sit here," said Adèle Hélene, dropping into an empty seat.

"I've been to France, you know," said Lizzie. "I've seen it all — the Eiffel Tower, Notre Dame, Euro Disney, Versailles. "

"My family has an apartment there," said Adèle Hélene.

"In Paris?"

"No, at Versailles. But it's a tiresome palace. I prefer my family's château."

"Do you?" said Lizzie in a bored voice.

"Where did you get those jeans?" asked Lizzie's friend, Vanessa Foster, eyeing the sapphires that dangled from the pocket of Adèle's pants.

"These? I get so many clothes I forget. But do you know where Katie Lexington shops?"

"No. Where?" said Lizzie and all her friends at once, leaning their heads in close.

Adèle Hélene paused dramatically, made sure that Josh was watching her, and announced sweetly, "SuperSaver."

"No!"

"Yes!"

A peal of giggles rang out across the room until Mrs. Pitney cleared her throat and quieted everyone down with a math assignment.

All morning long, Adèle Hélene exchanged titters and whispers with the girls around her, somehow managing to escape the notice of Mrs. Pitney. "Look at that lovely handwriting," the teacher declared, picking up Adèle Hélene's writing assignment. "It's a shame we don't stress handwriting in this country anymore." Adèle Hélene kept her eyes modestly lowered as she accepted the praise.

In the hall on the way to lunch, however, she pulled her hair back tightly and did a remarkably accurate imitation of Mrs. Pitney. "I've never had a prune for a tutor." She giggled and all the other girls surrounding her joined in. Then she waltzed off to lunch with them, leaving Josh staring after her.

"Your new exchange student is really, really pretty," Neil said to Josh after the girls left.

"You think?" said Josh. "I think she's the phoniest thing I ever met."

"A person can be phony *and* pretty," answered Neil.

Katie was waiting for Josh when he and Neil arrived in the cafeteria, and she was furious. "Excuse us, Neil," she said, dragging Josh over to a corner. "What are you doing? Here I am munching on my sandwich and what do I see? Our new Time Flyer surrounded by Lizzie Markle and her entire clique of snoopy girls. Lizzie's already onto the Time Flyers program! She'll sic Immigration on us again. The next thing you know, we'll be on the cover of one of those magazines in the supermarket next to a story about aliens, and we probably won't ever get to go back in time to see Jack or Kahotep or Humility." Katie stopped to catch her breath.

"Believe me, sis," said Josh, shaking his head. "That's not the problem."

"What do you mean?" fumed Katie.

"It's not what Lizzie Markle knows about Adèle Hélene that I'm worried about. It's what Lizzie Markle knows about *us*." And just at that moment, the entire gaggle of sixth-grade girls looked over at Katie and Josh and burst out laughing. Adèle Hélene raised a single eyebrow, smirked, and leaned in closer to gossip with her new friends.

Katie stared at them. "What's she been saying?" she asked Josh.

"Well, I couldn't catch it all, but she hates my sneakers. And she mentioned that Mom buys our clothes at SuperSaver."

Katie went white. "But she doesn't. I mean . . . she did for Adèle Hélene because why spend a lot of money on someone who's only here for a few days? Well, I mean, sometimes she gets stuff there. But so what? Everybody does."

"I don't know," said Josh. "I can't ever understand girls. And I like my sneakers just the way they are, thank you. I'm going to go eat lunch with Neil."

"And I'm going to go give that girl a piece of my mind." Katie took a deep breath and headed over to Adèle Hélene's table.

"Mind if I sit down?" Katie said firmly.

Adèle Hélene looked utterly surprised to see Katie standing there. "Oh, hi!" she gushed. "We were just talking about you." Vanessa Foster and Laurie Macavoy covered their mouths, trying not to laugh.

"Mind if I sit down?" said Katie again, with an even stronger voice.

"I wish you could, *Petit Rien*," said Adèle Hélene. The other girls repeated the nickname *Petit Rien* to one another and tittered. "But there just doesn't seem to be any room."

"No room," echoed Lizzie, spreading out her food.

"Someone's sitting here already." Vanessa and Laurie giggled, putting their hands on the empty seats beside them.

"We'll talk later," said Adèle Hélene to Katie. "Au revoir." She waved at Katie and turned away.

Katie looked around the bustling cafeteria. Kids were talking and trading sandwiches. Josh and Neil were playing cards while they snacked on chips. Her friends Kelly and Marissa were at the same table where they always ate lunch. She headed toward them and, for the first time, really noticed the kids who were sitting by themselves, reading books or just staring off into space.

"Hey, Sarah," she said to one girl who looked particularly alone. "Why don't you come sit with us?"

The girl looked up at her, startled at first, and then smiled.

4 FUN AND GAMES

"I love the telephone! *C'est fantastique!*"

All afternoon, Adèle Hélene had been lounging on Katie's bed talking on the phone to Lizzie Markle and a host of other girls. Every time the phone rang, Katie or Josh would have to leave their homework, answer it, and shout, "It's for you, Adèle Hélene."

"She sure made a lot of friends today," said Mrs. Lexington, looking up from the Christmas cards she was writing.

"At least it keeps her busy," said Josh. He punched the numbers on his calculator particularly hard.

"Four more days," said Katie grimly.

"It can't possibly be that many," muttered their mother, pausing for a moment to count. "Oh, my, I guess it is. You know, I realize I don't have any addresses for our Time Flyers. I do miss Jack in particular. He was such a nice boy. And dear Kahotep. And helpful Humility. Really, most of the children we've had have been so rewarding. I'll send their Christmas cards to the program and see if Mr. Dee can forward them on."

Adèle Hélene sauntered back into the dining room where they were all working, still holding the cordless phone. "What a hectic day," she said, sinking elegantly into a chair.

"You should get your homework done," said Josh. "Even if you are only here for the week, Mrs. Pitney will expect you to do it."

"Neil is doing it for me," explained Adèle Hélene. "I arranged it before I left school."

Disgusted, Josh slammed his math book shut. "Mom, I'm going outside to throw some snow-balls against trees." Mrs. Lexington gave him a sympathetic nod.

Katie continued working on her essay for Mrs.

Chandler while Adèle Hélene tapped her foot and hummed a tune. "So . . ." she finally said. "Are there to be any entertainments at all this evening? A trip to the theater? A musicale? A ball, perhaps?"

"It's a school night," said Mrs. Lexington, startled. "But maybe we can all play cards after dinner."

"Oh, well, that's something, isn't it?" Adèle Hélene sighed to no one in particular. She was idly fingering her hourglass necklace as if she already wanted to go home. "By the way, I'll be dining tomorrow night at the Markles. I'm going shopping with Lizzie in the afternoon."

"Oh," said Mrs. Lexington. "Will Katie be going with you?

"I'm not sure there's room in the carriage," said Adèle Hélene.

"It's fine, Mom," said Katie. "Believe me, I don't want to go."

"Well, I guess I'd better start dinner," said Mrs. Lexington, gathering up her cards.

As soon as she was out of the room, Katie turned on Adèle Hélene. "You better not let Lizzie know you're from the past. We're all going to be in big trouble if you do."

"I'm just going shopping with her, Katie. What do you expect me to do while I'm here, watch you scribble while your mother peels potatoes? I want to have a little fun. Also, I need some more clothes if I'm going to make it through the week. You can't expect me to wear the same thing every day. I came dreadfully unprepared for these modern fashions."

"What are you going to use for money?" asked Katie.

"Don't the stores accept credit? All the shops in Paris take credit from the better families. I never pay for anything."

"We have credit cards now — for everybody, not just the 'better' families."

"How do you get one of these credit cards?"

"Grown-ups have them. Not kids. Give it up, Adèle Hélene. You can look in the shop windows with Lizzie, but you can't buy anything, all right? And don't tell her anything!"

"*Petit Rien*, one of the first things you learn at

Court is always to know more about others than they know about you. Believe me, Lizzie Markle has no idea who I really am."

During dinner Adèle Hélene picked at her food. She peeled back the layers of the lasagna Mrs. Lexington had made, examined them, put down her knife and fork, and sipped from her water glass for the rest of the meal. "No one I know actually eats tomatoes," she finally said. Clearly irritated, Mrs. Lexington offered Josh and Katie seconds, and they both made a point of complimenting their mother on how good dinner was.

"Humility loved your lasagna, Mom," added Katie, referring to their last Time Flyer.

"Bet you're used to some good food in France," said Mr. Lexington cheerfully. "Eat a lot of French fries?"

"Excuse me, monsieur?"

"French fries," repeated Mr. Lexington. "Bet they're pretty tasty in France."

Adèle Hélene raised a single eyebrow. "Are you speaking of some kind of food?"

"You know, French fries. Maybe you don't call them that. Long, thin pieces of potato, deep-fried and salted."

"Potato? I tried one once, but I did not much like it."

"I would have thought everybody in France liked French fries," said Mr. Lexington, shaking his head. "But I've got a special treat for dessert that I'm pretty sure you will like." He left the table, went to the front hall, and came back with a gold-wrapped box. "I got us some special chocolates, in honor of your visit."

"Chocolates! I do love chocolates!" exclaimed Adèle Hélene. "Monsieur, you are too, too sweet!" She gave Mr. Lexington a glowing smile and he beamed back at her. She ripped open the box and immediately began sampling different pieces, biting into one and then another until she found one with a center she liked.

"Hey, leave some for us!" said Katie.

"Oh," said Adèle Hélene. "Here." She held out the box grudgingly and then returned it to her lap once Katie and Josh had taken some. "Now, didn't you promise we'd play some cards?" she asked between bites.

"I guess I did." Mrs. Lexington sighed.

"What a good idea, Betsy," said Mr. Lexington. "But you better watch out, Adèle Hélene. I'm a pretty good player!"

"I'm sure you are, *Monsieur Poulet*." Adèle Hélene smiled. "I'm sure you are."

Usually, Katie and Josh enjoyed a game of hearts or spades with their parents, but with Adèle Hélene hogging the chocolates and pouting whenever she lost, they were soon ready for bed.

"Oh, c'mon, kids. Let's play another round," said Mr. Lexington, who loved cards. "We've got to give Adèle Hélene a chance. She didn't even know the rules when she began!"

"I am not very good at cards, I'm afraid." Adèle Hélene sighed dramatically. "Perhaps we could play a game I know. I will teach you faro; it is the game of kings."

"Sounds fun!" said Mr. Lexington.

"I'm going to bed," said Josh. "I've had it."

"Me, too," said Katie.

"But it's not even close to your bedtime, kids," commented Mr. Lexington. "This is a great opportunity for you to learn something about France."

"Let them go," said Adèle Hélene, waving her hand dismissively. "You and I can play a game for grown-ups. Do you ever gamble, monsieur? It's so much more interesting to gamble."

"We're not really a gambling family," said Mrs. Lexington, giving her husband a sharp look.

"Betsy here won't even let me buy lottery tickets," admitted Mr. Lexington.

"We don't need to play for high stakes," said Adèle Hélene, already beginning to deal the cards.

"Abner." Mrs. Lexington glared at her husband just before she went upstairs. "Be careful."

"Don't worry, honey! I'll go easy on her."

"I just hope your father knows what he's doing," Mrs. Lexington whispered to Katie on the stairs.

"Me, too, Mom. Me, too." But just before she headed to bed, Katie glanced one more time at the table and saw Adèle Hélene shuffling the cards masterfully and dealing them like she'd grown up at a casino.

The next morning, Mr. Lexington hurried off to work without even a second cup of coffee.

"What's the matter with Dad?" asked Josh, pouring himself a bowl of cereal.

"He wouldn't say," Mrs. Lexington said grimly. "But I have my suspicions." She looked at the calendar on the refrigerator and sighed. "Three more days."

On the way out the door, Josh noticed Adèle Hélene quietly slipping something green into her coat pocket.

"What is she holding?" whispered Josh to Katie.

"Oh, no! I can't believe it," said Katie.

"What?" asked Josh.

"It's a credit card. She won Dad's credit card."

Adèle Hélene smiled, her eyes sparkling. "And, for once, I didn't even need to cheat."

5 SMALL TALK

By the end of the week, Adèle Hélene was unquestionably the most popular girl at Alice R. Quigley Middle School.

She had come home from her shopping trip with Lizzie with bags and bags of clothes, jewelry, accessories, and shoes. She had handed Mr. Lexington his credit card with a sweet smile. "*Merci*, monsieur," she'd said to him before Mrs. Lexington dragged him upstairs and slammed the door.

The next day, Adèle Hélene was surrounded by girls the moment she got on the bus, all eager to sit near her and compliment her on her outfit. In class, she passed notes to Lizzie and her gang that made them have to hide their laughter from Mrs. Pitney. She sweet-talked the cafeteria ladies so they gave her free cookies, charmed Mrs. Pitney until she got a pass to go anywhere in the building, waved at the secretaries in the office, and waltzed through the halls attracting admiring stares from the children in lower grades. She gave endearing little nicknames to everyone. Lizzie was *Le Grand Bouton* and the other girls in their group, *Le Petit Chien* and *La Vache Laide*. She called Mr. Tufnell, their chorus teacher, Monsieur Corneille. "What does it mean?" he asked her.

"You sing like a bird, sir," she answered sweetly. "Like a bird."

Mr. Tufnell cleared his throat, looking very pleased. "Well, we are lucky to have you with us. You, too, sing like a bird. Like a nightingale. Your voice sounds positively trained."

"Yes, I can warble a bit. I have had a tutor since I was five." She fluttered her eyelashes prettily.

"I only wish you were going to be here for the holiday concert! I'd love to give you a solo. Do you really have to leave us on Friday?"

"I suppose," pouted Adèle Hélene.

"And it's too bad you can't come to my party after the concert. I always have the best holiday party," added Lizzie. "Everyone comes."

"I'm sure *le Bouton* and her darling mother throw the most divine fetes," gushed Adèle Hélene.

Josh made a gagging gesture to Neil, but Neil didn't notice. He was mesmerized by Adèle Hélene, his eyes wide, his mouth hanging open. "Don't drool, Neil. Please," begged Josh.

On Friday afternoon, Katie met secretly with Josh in his room. "I think we are the only two people who are going to be happy to see her go."

"Mom, too, " said Josh. "She's been marking off the days in her date book. I caught her at it."

"Here's my question," whispered Katie, checking to make sure the door was shut. "Do you think we should tell her about the French Revolution before she goes? I know she's totally annoying, but the guillotine does seem like a horrible fate to send her back to."

"That girl's going to survive, Katie. I mean,

she's got the Pit Bull eating out of her hand. She gets whatever she wants." Josh rolled over on his bed. "She'll be fine."

"Still . . ." Katie had read about the horrible riots and the families thrown into prison and executed and Josh hadn't. It was one thing to not like someone; it was another to wish a revolution on them.

She went back to her room, where Adèle Hélene was admiring herself in front of the mirror. "Can I talk to you for a minute?" said Katie.

"Girl talk?" asked Adèle Hélene. "You know, Katie, I've been wanting to talk to *you* for some time. Come." She sat down on the bed, and patted a spot beside her for Katie to sit. "First of all, I'm telling you this because I'm your friend. That's why I'm so concerned about how you dress. When I first came here, I thought maybe nobody cared about fashion in the future, but I've since learned that most of the girls do. Oh, Katie, I just don't want you to go into sixth grade looking like this."

"There is more to life than clothes, Adèle Hélene," said Katie through clenched teeth.

"But, of course!" said Adèle Hélene. "That is exactly why I was also going to tell you to get your ears pierced."

Katie balled her hands into fists and took a deep breath. "Adèle Hélene, I've got to tell you something before you go back to the eighteenth century tomorrow."

Adèle Hélene sighed and picked up a hairbrush. "Oh, Katie, you can be so tiresome sometimes."

"Tiresome? Adèle Hélene, you could be in horrible danger when you go home," snapped Katie. "The peasants are going to storm the Bastille and imprison the king and queen and start killing everybody. Is that really tiresome?"

"Whatever are you talking about?" asked Adèle Hélene, continuing to brush her hair.

"There's going to be a revolution in France not long after you get home."

Adèle Hélene burst out laughing. "Oh, you are just like those old scolds in the corners of Versailles.

'The peasants are hungry. The harvest was bad. The order must be changed.' It's all such a bore. Besides," said Adèle Hélene slyly, "I'm not sure I *am* going back."

"What?" said Katie, forgetting all about the French Revolution. "That's not a choice. You're going back tomorrow. You *have* to."

Adèle Hélene tossed her shimmering hair. "Oh, I think not. I'm beginning to like life in the United States of America, the malls in particular."

Katie couldn't believe it. It wasn't possible. Their Time Flyers always went back. They had to. What would happen if they didn't? Katie watched Adèle Hélene put on a pair of earrings and primp in front of the mirror. And then she realized that Adèle Hélene wasn't wearing her hourglass necklace!

"Where's your necklace?" asked Katie sharply.

"Oh!" Adèle Hélene sighed. "It was so ugly, wasn't it? I'm glad to be rid of it. I think these rhinestones Lizzie gave me are so much prettier. I love all these fake jewels. It's really remarkable how real they look."

Katie jumped off the bed and started looking

around the room in Adèle Hélene's overflowing trunks and bags. "Where is it? It's the only way you can travel through time! You've got to put it back on."

"Do I?" asked Adèle Hélene, one eyebrow raised.

"Otherwise you can't go home!"

"Precisely," said Adèle Hélene. "It looks like I'm staying right here."

6 HANGERS ON

"Not going back? Not going back? But that's against the rules!" Josh was frantic. He had been relaxing in his room, listening to music and playing with his Game Boy when Katie barged in with the bad news. "I'll hold her down if you want, and you can wrap the hourglass around her neck. She only has to be touching it to go back, right?"

"Yup," said Katie. "She just has to be touching it. But we don't know where it is. She's hidden it."

"Oh, no!" groaned Josh. "We have to tell Mom!"

"Sure," said Katie. "We'll tell her that the nice

little student exchange program is really magic and the kids come from back in time and we need to find the golden hourglass to send Adèle Hélene home. Right. She'll be calling the school counselor before you know it."

"Still," said Josh. "We have to figure out some way of getting her to e-mail Mr. Dee. This is a catastrophe. I can't bring that girl to school with me one more day."

Their mother was in the living room wrapping presents for relatives when they came downstairs. Katie watched her tie off the last ribbon before she said anything. "Mom, we've got bad news."

"What, sweetheart?" Mrs. Lexington unfurled another piece of paper and began to cut it.

"Adèle Hélene isn't going back tomorrow," said Katie.

"And she has to," added Josh. "She really has to."

"Of course she's going back," said Mrs. Lexington. "Tomorrow. Mr. Dee assured me by e-mail she's going back tomorrow."

"What's this about Adèle Hélene?" said Mr. Lexington, coming into the room. He had been outside putting up more holiday lights.

"She's not going back," Katie said.

"That's great!" said Mr. Lexington, dropping into a chair. "You know, I've had my doubts about this Time Flyers program, but we're really getting some special kids. Why, this girl is practically royalty."

"A royal pain," muttered Katie to herself.

But there was no convincing her mother to contact Mr. Dee — at least not until the next evening, when Adèle Hélene was stretched out on the couch, a cell phone in her hand, chatting away about Lizzie's upcoming party. "No, *really*? I had no idea she did that. Of course she can't come," she was saying to some girl on the other line.

"Your father's gone out to get a tree and I thought we'd decorate it tonight," whispered Mrs. Lexington to Katie and Josh. "After she's gone."

"She's not going, Mom. I warned you," said Katie.

"Usually the program is so prompt. Overly prompt. I mean, I never even had a chance to say good-bye to our last three guests. They just seemed to disappear."

"Can you please e-mail Mr. Dee now, Mom?" urged Josh. "We've got to figure this out. Otherwise I'm not going to school anymore. On Friday, Adèle Hélene told Evan and Frank that I still had a teddy bear in my room."

"What's the matter with having a teddy bear in your room, dear?"

"Mom!" said Josh, exasperated. "Just go upstairs to your office right now and write to Mr. Dee."

While their mother went up to her computer, Katie turned to Adèle Hélene. "We need to talk."

"I've got to go," Adèle Hélene said into the phone, obviously irritated. "*Le Petit Rien* and her brother have some little problem. I know, I know, I can't believe he wears them, either. . . . Au revoir."

"You've got to go home, now!" Katie said after

Adèle hung up. "Who knows how you might mess up history if you don't go back."

"Mmm." Adèle Hélene traced the pattern of an embroidered pillow with her finger. "I have been thinking about that."

"Is it Katie's fault?" asked Josh. "Did she scare you with all that revolution talk? 'Cause you still have plenty of time to go home and escape with your parents."

"Yeah," chimed in Katie. "Don't you want to go home and see your parents?"

"My parents, Katie, are in for an interesting little surprise. They had planned to wed me next month to the grandson of Le Marechal du Crainon, but it seems as though the bride in question may be unavailable for the ceremony."

"Married?" said Josh, shocked. "But you're only twelve."

"So?" said Adèle Hélene. "The queen was only thirteen when she left Austria. And my friend Marguerite was betrothed when she was eleven. Tragically, le marechal's grandson was scarred by the pox. He has sores all over his face, but still, it is quite an income."

Just then Mr. Lexington came into the room carrying an enormous Christmas tree. "Close the door for me, will you, Josh?" panted their father, resting the tree against the wall. "Whew! That was heavy. Hey, Adèle Hélene, I'm glad you're still here. I was afraid I might have missed you."

"Adèle Hélene isn't going home for quite some time, Abner," announced Mrs. Lexington, coming downstairs. She shook her head. "Adèle Hélene, that was not very thoughtful of you to miss your appointed meeting time with Mr. Dee. He's going to have some difficulty making additional travel plans now. The holidays are a very hectic time of year, and it looks like you may be spending them with us. I wrote Mr. Dee that I'd be happy to drive you to the airport, but apparently it's not possible to get a last-minute flight."

"That's a fact, Betsy," said Mr. Lexington. "It's a busy time of year to fly."

"But I'd drive her to *any* airport," Mrs.

Lexington insisted. "It doesn't matter how many hours away it is. It's no inconvenience. I'd pay for it myself."

"I'm not sure we can do that," said Mr. Lexington. "Now, who wants to help me get this tree in the stand?" Josh went over to lend a hand.

"Dad doesn't get it, does he?" said Katie to her mother.

"No," answered Mrs. Lexington. "He's a sweet man, your father. We'll just have to cope." She looked at Adèle Hélene and sighed. "We've already spent so much on that girl's clothes, I can't imagine what we're going to give her for Christmas, and Mr. Dee can't even tell me when she's going to go back. Apparently, she was supposed to have already left but refused. What a nuisance!"

Katie was mad, too, but all she could think about that night while they showed Adèle Hélene how to decorate a Christmas tree was what it must be like to get married before you were even a teenager. "Does everybody get married so young?" she asked, handing Adèle Hélene an ornament.

"*Non*. But my father has so many gambling debts. He had hoped to win the king's lottery, but alas 'twas not so. Le marechal's grandson will bring us fifty thousand a year."

"Hey, Adèle," interrupted Mr. Lexington. "Why don't you put up the angel? She looks like you!"

"*Merci, Monsieur Poulet*." She smiled. "I do like this tradition of a decorated tree. It is very lovely. And your little house has been transformed." Not only did the tree glitter with ornaments and lights, but Mrs. Lexington had hung mistletoe, set up nutcrackers and snow globes around the room, and put beautiful red bows and pine garlands on the staircase. "*C'est très belle!*" said Adèle Hélene, clapping her hands.

"Just you wait until we make our gingerbread house and holiday cookies!" beamed Mrs. Lexington. She was always very proud of how her home looked at Christmas.

"Do you cook foods for Noel?" asked Adèle Hélene.

"Oh, yes, dear. Katie and I have some real

specialties. Wait until you try our chocolate truffles. We give them as gifts every year to our friends."

"Madame Lexington?" asked Adèle Hélene. "I have such a lovely idea."

"Yes, dear?" answered Mrs. Lexington. She was fussing with the placement of an ornament and moving it to a higher branch.

"I just wish everyone could see how beautiful your house looks. . . ."

Mrs. Lexington looked at Adèle Hélene. "That's sweet of you to say so."

"I think that's the first nice thing she's said about our family since she arrived," muttered Josh to Katie.

"Mmm," said Katie to Josh. "Maybe." Adèle Hélene was whispering something in Mrs. Lexington's ear and giggling. Mrs. Lexington was nodding her head and smiling.

"Children, Adèle Hélene has come up with the most wonderful idea. She thinks we should throw a holiday party for your classmates. We can do it as a celebration after the holiday music concert. Wouldn't that be fun?"

Yup, thought Katie, *now I know what she was up to.* "Isn't Lizzie Markle giving a party that night?" she asked.

"Is she?" asked Mrs. Lexington.

"Not anymore, I'm afraid," said Adèle Hélene, gazing at her reflection in an ornament and smiling. "Not anymore."

7 RSVP (REPONDEZ S'IL VOUS PLAÎT)

Lizzie was handing out invitations to *her* party the next morning in Josh's class. They were in red and green envelopes with little candy canes attached to them.

"Ooh, I can't wait," squealed Vanessa as she opened hers. "I'm going to get a special dress."

"These invitations are adorable," cooed Laurie.

Lizzie handed an invitation to Adèle Hélene. "I'm so excited that you're staying in America now and can come. Now *everyone*'s going to be there!" Then she frowned at Josh. "I was going to invite you and your sister, but my mother says I can only invite so many kids. Maybe next time, okay?"

Josh wasn't sure why Adèle Hélene didn't mention the party she was planning on giving, but he decided that he really couldn't be bothered to figure it out. Girls were strange. Besides, Mrs. Pitney was now yelling at Lizzie for handing out invitations in school. "It's not nice and it's not fair to your other classmates," the Pit Bull scolded.

But Lizzie just rolled her eyes.

At chorus that day, Mr. Tufnell was so thrilled to discover that Adèle Hélene would be participating in the holiday concert that he spilled his coffee all over his attendance book. "That voice! That voice!" he exclaimed as he cleaned up the mess. "What a concert we're going to have this year!"

"And what a party afterward," said Lizzie.

Adèle Hélene just hummed a tune to herself. Only at lunch later that day did Josh notice her pulling Laurie and Vanessa aside and whispering intently with them. And that afternoon, notes went back and forth between the girls in class.

"What are you all going on about?" Lizzie asked.

"Just what to wear to the party," said Adèle Hélene, innocently, and Laurie and Vanessa both burst out laughing.

That evening, while Josh and Katie worked on their homework at the dining room table, Adèle Hélene assembled paper, watercolors, ribbons, and markers.

"Wow," said Katie, admiring the invitations Adèle was creating. "Those paintings and the letters are amazing. They are really beautiful." On each invitation, Adèle Hélene had created a perfect picture of the Lexington's holiday-decorated house. Underneath each picture, in gold letters was written, *"Adèle Hélene Marie Louise Marguerite de la Bouche requests your presence at supper on the evening of December 19th...."* Adèle was folding each invitation carefully and wrapping it with a ribbon.

"I'd love to have everyone to Papa's château," she said. "As it is, I don't think we'll be able to fit everyone in this house."

"I think just the fifth and sixth graders," said Mrs. Lexington, coming into the room. "And dear Mr. Tufnell, of course. That's a big enough group."

"Yes, you never want to invite too many people to a party," agreed Adèle Hélene.

When her mother had gone back to the kitchen, Katie turned to Adèle Hélene. Something had been bothering her. "Do you have to marry this boy your parents have set up for you?" she asked.

"But, of course," said Adèle Hélene. "If I do not, Papa will send me to a convent. He has promised to do so. And that would be so terribly dull."

"Don't you get any say in who you marry?" asked Josh. "I mean, can't you pick somebody you like?"

For a moment, an expression of sadness passed across Adèle Hélene's face, but almost instantly she recovered from it. She shrugged her shoulders. "How unfashionable! Nobody loves their husband. My mother never spends any time with my father at all."

"Our mom loves our dad," said Josh. From

the kitchen they could all hear the sound of Mr. and Mrs. Lexington laughing together while they did the dishes.

"I've noticed," said Adèle Hélene. The same darkness welled up in her eyes again, but she threw back her shoulders and shrugged. "It's so sweet," she said dismissively.

The next morning, Adèle Hélene carefully put her invitations in her backpack. "You're not supposed to give those out in school," said Katie as they headed to the bus.

"Of course," said Adèle Hélene. "Do you think I'd be so foolish? As it is, Mrs. Pitney adores me."

Only at lunch did Katie figure out what Adèle Hélene was up to. Neil Carmody walked around the cafeteria handing out the invitations. Squeals of delight came from various tables after Neil passed by, and Katie couldn't help watching for Lizzie's reaction.

"Are you going?" Josh asked Neil as he passed their table.

"I don't know. She told me if some kids didn't come she might have room for me. But it was really nice of her to let me give out the cards, wasn't it?"

"Neil, you are hopeless," said Josh.

"She's even given me a nickname," admitted Neil.

"What?" asked Katie.

"She calls me *Derrière du Cochon*. Isn't that cool? Doesn't it sound royal?"

"Maybe," Katie said, while Josh made a gagging noise.

Just at that moment, Lizzie stormed over to Neil. "What are you handing out?" she demanded. "Give those to me."

"I can't," said Neil, backing up. "I don't have one for you."

Lizzie grabbed an invitation out of his hand and tore it open. Quickly she read what it said. Then she read it again. And again. Her face was getting redder and redder and redder.

"Watch out," whispered Josh to Katie. "I think she's gonna blow."

Lizzie stormed over to where Adèle Hélene sat, surrounded by all the popular girls. "How could you plan *your* party for the same night as *my* party? I always have my party the night of the holiday concert," she screamed. "And you haven't even invited me!"

Adèle Hélene observed her without any reaction at all. "How could I invite someone with so little self-control?" she asked her friends. "Really."

The other girls burst out laughing, so Lizzie stomped over to Katie and Josh. "This is all your fault. Your exchange students, if that's what they really are, always ruin everything. Everything!"

"But they're not invited, either," said Neil.

"What?" said Lizzie.

"I don't have an invitation for Josh or Katie here." He looked over the remaining invitations in his hand. "Nope. Nothing."

"But it's at our house," said Katie. "We don't need an invitation. We're *giving* the party."

"That's not what it says," said Lizzie. "It says, 'Adèle Hélene whatever whatever requests your presence . . .' There's nothing here about the Lexingtons. Your name isn't even on the card."

"It doesn't matter," said Josh. "It's at our house. It's our party technically. We're invited."

"But not as guests," Adèle Hélene said simply.

"What are we, then? Servants?" said Katie.

"Yes. Yes, *Petit Rien*. Exactly." Adèle Hélene smiled. "Oh, I'm so glad you understand. I've scheduled a training session for your family this weekend. Your mother will, of course, stay in the kitchen, but I will need the two of you to serve and take coats. And, Katie, you can be upstairs to help girls with their hair. I've already discussed it with your father. He's so excited about being a valet."

Josh couldn't believe it. "We haven't been invited to our own party?"

"Oh, Joshua," said Adèle Hélene, shaking her head. "How could I invite you when you're still wearing those terrible sneakers? It would ruin everything." And with that she tossed her hair and walked out of the cafeteria, surrounded by her friends.

Josh and Katie stood there absolutely speechless, as all around them children packed up their lunches and left the cafeteria. Only Lizzie Markle was left beside them.

"I can't believe it," said Katie finally. "I just can't believe that girl."

"She has got to go back to France," fumed Josh. "Now."

"Definitely," said Lizzie. "Wasn't she supposed to go back a few days ago?"

Josh and Katie both nodded their heads.

"Then why didn't she go?" asked Lizzie.

"She lost something," said Katie. "A necklace."

"A really expensive necklace," added Josh. "Irreplaceable."

"Then we better find it," said Lizzie. "The sooner the better. Like yesterday."

8 NAME TAGS

Katie had searched all of Adèle Hélene's trunks and jewelry boxes. Josh had looked in every drawer and closet, and even under the cushions of the couch. Lizzie had skipped lunch and managed to rummage through Adèle Hélene's desk and locker. "How did you open the lock?" asked Katie.

"That?" Lizzie shrugged. "That's easy."

But they hadn't found the hourglass necklace.

Now they had gotten their father to take them all to the mall, where they planned to spy on Adèle Hélene. She was already there with Vanessa and Laurie. "We'll meet up with you at the food court in an hour. Okay, Dad?" said Josh.

"You bet," said Mr. Lexington. "I've got a few more Christmas surprises to pick up. "

The three kids took off in the opposite direction to find Adèle Hélene. "What are we going to do when we find those girls, anyway?" asked Josh.

"Listen," said Lizzie, peering into stores as they walked. "She's given that necklace to Vanessa or Laurie. I just know it. We need to hear her talking about it when she doesn't think we're around. She's very sneaky."

"Takes one to know one," muttered Josh to Katie.

Eventually, they found the three girls with Vanessa's mother in an upscale boutique. They slunk in, careful not to be seen, and crouched behind a rack of sweaters. Vanessa, Laurie, and Adèle Hélene were trying on jewelry a few feet away. "Oh, I just love this bracelet with pink stones, don't you, *mon Chien*?" exclaimed Adèle Hélene.

"You look so pretty in it. You just have to get it," said Vanessa.

"You'll get it for me, right?"

Vanessa hesitated.

"Pretty please, *Petit Chien*?" begged Adèle Hélene. "I'll get you something special when you visit me in Paris."

"Okay, I'll ask my mom," said Vanessa. "Mom!" she shouted, and within minutes Vanessa's mother was pulling out her credit card for all kinds of jewelry and clothes at the cash register.

"I can't believe they're actually buying her all this stuff," whispered Katie to the others.

"Why?" said Lizzie. "She's fabulously wealthy. She has castles and diamonds and hangs out with royalty. She'll pay it all back at some point. Anyway, that's what she told my mother and me."

"Yeah?" said Josh. "Let's just say it's a lot more complicated than you can possibly imagine, getting money from there to here."

"Sssh!" said Katie. "Listen."

"I'm so sorry, girls, but I don't lend out *any* of my jewelry," Adèle Hélene was saying to

Laurie as they all walked out of the store. "Most of it's a gift from the queen. You understand, don't you?"

"Oh, I completely understand," said Laurie quickly. "After all, the queen. Tell us again about the time you danced with her son."

"Not now, *Vache Laide*. Not now."

Vanessa giggled. "I love when you call me that. It's so . . . so . . . so French!"

Lizzie looked hurt for a moment. "She used to call me *le Grand Bouton*. It sounds so cool and important," she said. "I guess we can just go home now. Now we know that Laurie and Vanessa don't have the necklace."

"How do we know that?" asked Josh.

Lizzie gave an exasperated sigh. "She told Laurie she didn't lend out her jewelry. And I believe her."

"I do, too," agreed Katie. "You know, if she did give them the necklace, there would always be the danger they might wear it at the wrong moment."

"What do you mean?" Lizzie asked sharply. "What is it about that necklace you're not telling me?"

Realizing that she'd nearly spilled the beans about the Time Flyers program to the one person who was most suspicious about it, Katie quickly changed the subject. "Oh, look, a bookstore. I need something in there. C'mon!" She grabbed Josh by the arm and raced toward the store.

"What are you doing?" panted Lizzie, running to catch up.

"Yeah, what are we doing?" said Josh.

Katie walked up and down the aisles until she found what she was looking for: a French–English dictionary. "Hey, guys," she said, motioning to Josh and Lizzie to come over. "Let's find out what everyone's nickname means. I've been wanting to know what she's been calling me for a long time."

"I'm looking mine up first," said Lizzie, grabbing the book out of Katie's hand. "*Grand Bouton, Grand Bouton*," she mumbled. Her finger ran down a list of words and stopped. Lizzie's eyes narrowed and she slammed the book shut. "That's it," she announced to Josh and Katie. "That girl has to go. And I mean it."

"Obviously," said Josh. "But what does your nickname mean?"

"None of your business," said Lizzie, shoving the book back onto the shelf.

"That cute, huh?" said Katie. "I *know* mine's going to be bad." She took out the dictionary and looked through it. "Now, I'm just guessing at spelling here, but I do believe she's been calling me 'Little Nothing.' Isn't that charming?"

"At least it's not 'Big Pimple!'" laughed Josh, who'd taken out another dictionary and looked up *Grand Bouton*.

"You tell one person what *Grand Bouton* means, Joshua Lexington, and tacky sneakers will be the least of your problems." Lizzie glared at Josh.

"Somebody please tell me . . . what is the matter with my sneakers?" asked Josh, looking down at his feet.

Katie just ignored him and went up to the counter to buy the dictionary. *I have a feeling this is going to come in handy*, she thought.

The three children left the bookstore and headed toward the food court, Lizzie walking a few feet in front of Josh and Katie in case she ran into someone she knew. On the way there, they nearly bumped into Neil Carmody, who was busy window-shopping. "What are you doing here?" Josh asked Neil.

Neil blushed. "My mom's getting her nails done, and I thought I might, you know, find a little something for Adèle Hélène."

"Hopeless," said Josh. "Absolutely hopeless."

"I'll say," added Lizzie, tossing her head. "I can't believe I'm hanging out with you people. Hey, what is it that Adèle Hélène calls you, anyway?"

Neil turned even redder and smiled shyly. "She calls me *Le Derrière du Cochon*. Doesn't it sound like the name of a duke or a general or something?"

"Look it up," Lizzie ordered Katie.

Katie thumbed through the dictionary. "Okay, I've got one of the words, I think." She continued looking, sounding out the word to herself. "Oh, Neil, I am so sorry."

"What? What?"

"Neil, don't buy that girl a present," said Katie, putting the dictionary back in the shopping bag.

"Tell me what it means in English, Katie," he pleaded.

"You don't want to know."

"I do! I do!"

"Okay. *Derrière* means 'behind'."

"Behind? Behind what?"

"Not that kind of behind, Neil. I think it's behind as in butt," said Josh.

"That's right, and *cochon* is 'pig'," finished Katie.

"So she thinks you're a pig's butt," said Lizzie.

"See what I mean?" said Josh. "Don't get her anything for Christmas."

Neil was crestfallen. "But I really thought she liked me. She even gave me a present."

"*What?*" all three kids said together.

"She gave me her most special necklace and asked me to keep it safe for her. She said it was because she could trust me. Why would she call me something awful like that? That book must be wrong. Or you're spelling it wrong or something."

"Does that necklace have a tiny gold hourglass hanging from it?" asked Katie.

"Yeah," said Neil. "How'd you know?"

9 LAST-MINUTE PLANS

Mrs. Lexington was just hanging up the telephone when Josh, Katie, and Lizzie arrived home from the mall. Her eyes were fiery. "Do you know that that is the eleventh phone call I have gotten this afternoon? Can you believe that girl didn't invite over half of the children in the holiday concert to the party? And now their parents are all calling me to find out why they were excluded. I've had it. She has to go back. I don't care how, but it has to be now. I'm about ready to row her in a boat across the ocean myself."

"I'll help you," said Lizzie.

"By the way, your mother called, too, Lizzie. I told her you could come whether you got an invitation or not. In fact, I'm calling everyone to tell them they are all welcome to come."

"The cool kids won't like that," said Lizzie. "They'll come to my party instead."

"The 'cool' kids may do whatever they like," Mrs. Lexington said sharply. "Your mother, Lizzie, is picking you up in ten minutes." She turned on Mr. Lexington, who was just coming into the kitchen with his arms full of shopping bags. "Abner, I hope you didn't spend any more money on Adèle Hélene."

"Just a couple stocking stuffers, Betsy . . ."

Mrs. Lexington banged the pot she was holding down on the counter. Katie, Josh, and Lizzie snuck upstairs to Katie's room before the conversation went any further.

"There's one thing I've been meaning to ask you," Lizzie said. "What's so important about that necklace? Why can't she go back without it? I remember Jack Bradford, your first exchange student, had one, too, and you were in an awful hurry to make sure he got it back. Why?"

Josh looked at Katie, hoping she knew what to say.

Katie bit her lip. "It's sort of like part of their passport," she began. "You know, they need it to get in and out of the country."

"That doesn't make any sense," said Lizzie, her eyes narrowing. "I've been out of the country. I didn't need any special necklace."

A car honked out in the driveway. "Lizzie, that's your mom," said Katie. Then, to change the subject, she added, "Why don't you take the dictionary? Translate all the girls' nicknames for them. That might convince Adèle Hélene it's time to go home."

"It just might," said Lizzie, brightening. "My party may not be ruined after all." She took the dictionary and ran out to the waiting car.

"Katie, can I ask you something, too?" said Josh when Lizzie was out of the room. "Are my sneakers really that ugly?"

Katie looked at her older brother affectionately and shook her head. "Do *you* like them?"

"Yeah. They're really comfortable."

"If *you* like them, that's the only thing that matters," Katie said. "Now let's get on Mom's computer while she's cooking dinner and see if we can contact Mr. Dee and let him know it's time to send Adèle Hélene home."

Katie and Josh had visited the Time Flyers Web site and checked out the program before. It was all completely ordinary-looking. Nothing on the site told you that the kids would be coming from back in time — except one small question on the application that asked about "your time preference." They weren't sure if they would be able to contact Mr. Dee, but they knew their mother did, so it had to be easy.

"There it is," said Josh, leaning over his sister's shoulder and pointing to a box at the bottom of the screen. "'*Contact.*' If you click that button, maybe an e-mail address will pop up."

Katie did it, and it worked. "What should we write?"

"Take her back," said Josh. "You can make it sound prettier than that, but I think that's the best Christmas present we can give Mom."

"And ourselves," said Katie.

She wrote a long e-mail explaining about how the necklace had been hidden and recently found. But while she was thinking about the politest way to ask to get rid of Adèle Hélene, an IM with an unfamiliar e-mail address popped up on the screen. *Josh and Katie, could you please direct your attention over here?* it read.

"Who's that from?" asked Josh.

"I don't know," said Katie.

A new message appeared on the screen: *You know me as Mr. Dee.*

"That's weird," said Josh. "It's almost like he heard us talking."

I can hear you, another message instantly answered. *I need you to pay careful attention to what I am about to write. This message will vanish as soon as you leave the room, and you must remember everything I tell you if Adèle Hélene is to stay out of danger. I have programmed the hourglass to return Adèle Hélene to her own century tomorrow night at 9:30 TFCST.*

"TFCST?" wondered Katie out loud.

Twenty-first Century Standard Time popped up on the screen.

Katie continued reading the message. *Adèle Hélene must be touching the necklace at 9:30. Otherwise, I may not be able to schedule her in for a number of years.*

"Years?" said Josh.

Years, responded a new IM. *But, please, no more interruptions. Our time is limited.*

You must also explain to Adèle Hélene that she will not be returning to 1789 as we had originally planned. Unfortunately, due to her disregard for the rules, the year will now be 1792. Katie can, I think, appreciate what this will mean for a French aristocrat. Tell her that when she returns to Versailles, she is to immediately go to the main gate, where a blue carriage will be waiting for her. She is to leave behind all her belongings except a cloak that she must use to cover her face. She is not to exit the carriage until I, myself, open the door. Her life depends upon it.

Can you remember all this?

"Yes," Katie and Josh answered.

I thought so. You are doing an excellent job. I am very proud of you both. And with that, all the IM messages vanished from the screen. A moment later, the entire computer completely shut down.

"Wow," said Josh. "That was really cool."

"But there's so much I wanted to ask him about the program," said Katie. "Like, will we ever get to go back in time? How? When?"

"I don't know," said Josh. "But I do know that if Adèle Hélene doesn't leave tomorrow, I'm going to have to switch schools, or maybe even families."

But Katie wasn't listening to Josh. She was looking at the blank screen and thinking hard about something.

"What's wrong, Katie?" Josh asked.

"Maybe we shouldn't send her back. . . ."

"What are you talking about?"

Katie bit her lip. "I've read about the French Revolution, Josh. You haven't. At first, it starts out okay, but then everything goes crazy. The time Adèle Hélene will be returning to? It's almost the Reign of Terror. All the aristocrats were getting their heads chopped off, even kids and old people. Probably a lot of people Adèle Hélene knows are already dead."

"But it sounds like Mr. Dee has a plan to help her escape."

"I know," said Katie. "But how good is that girl at following rules? She thinks she can do whatever she wants. What if something goes wrong? What will happen to her?"

A door slammed downstairs. Adèle Hélene was home from the mall. They heard her musical voice sing out, "Madame Lexington, I'm going to relax in a bath and you can serve me my supper in bed, *s'il vous plaît*." Adèle Hélene passed Katie and Josh on her way to the bedroom. "Ah! There you are. I still haven't gone over with you what I want you to do tomorrow night, Katie. You are up, I think, to being a maid."

Katie ignored Adèle, rolling her eyes. "So this is what we have to figure out," Katie explained to

Josh after Adèle Hélene walked on. "Somehow we need to tell her about the plans without letting on that we are actually sending her back."

"Right," said Josh. "I think I know how to do it."

10 SURPRISE

Adèle Hélene was in a hurry to get home after the concert. She had dazzled everyone with her solo during the medley of holiday favorites, but she was in no mood to collect praise from parents in the lobby. "I need to be back before everyone arrives so I can change my outfit. *Allons-y!*" she snapped at Mr. Lexington, practically dragging him to the parking lot.

In the car she started issuing more directions. "Josh and Katie, you may keep on your chorus outfits. I like the black and white. Mrs. Lexington, perhaps you could change into something a little more, shall we say, subdued?"

Mrs. Lexington cleared her throat but didn't

say anything. She was wearing her favorite green velvet skirt and a red sweater decorated with a mistletoe pattern.

It had started to snow lightly and as they came up the driveway, Adèle Hélene instructed Mr. Lexington to sweep off the walkway before everyone arrived. "And why don't you stay out here and see to people's carriages."

"Good idea!" said Mr. Lexington cheerfully. "You sure do think of everything, young lady."

"Not everything," whispered Josh to Katie.

"Let's hope not," she answered.

Adèle Hélene was still fussing with her hair when the first guests started pulling into the driveway. She glided down the stairs as she heard the door opening, an entrancing smile on her face that slowly faded away as she saw who was standing in the hallway. It was Neil Carmody and a few of his friends. "What are you doing here?" she gasped. "I didn't invite you."

"No, but I did." Mrs. Lexington emerged from the kitchen, a platter of cookies in her hands. "C'mon, c'mon in everyone! Cocoa's ready!"

More kids had arrived and were taking off their hats and coats and trooping into the living room. Brian Bucar, one of Katie's fifth-grade classmates, showed up with a Twister game and spread it out on the floor. Neil Carmody was trying to balance a candy cane on his nose.

"*Non! Non! Non!*" shrieked Adèle Hélene. "None of you have been invited! You must leave this minute!" She ran outside and told Mr. Lexington not to let anyone inside without an invitation.

"We won't worry about that!" he said. "You can't turn anyone away at Christmas. That's not the holiday spirit."

Just at that moment, Laurie and Vanessa got out of a car. They had changed out of their chorus clothes and were wearing what were obviously brand-new outfits. Vanessa's lip curled as she looked around her. "Who are all these kids?" she asked Adèle Hélene.

"Yeah," added Laurie. "I thought you said this party was just for our friends."

"Mikey and Ben and the other kids are gonna flip when they see who's here," said Vanessa.

Adèle Hélene threw up her hands in despair. "All was so perfectly planned. I do not know what has happened."

"Hi, everybody!" cried Lizzie Markle from the driveway, carrying a pile of presents in her arms. "I thought I'd drop by here for a little bit, and then I'm heading back to my own party. Just to let you know."

Vanessa and Laurie exchanged a knowing look and followed Lizzie inside.

"Look who's here!" said Josh to Katie.

"Time for a game of Secret Santa," announced Katie. "Gather around, everybody."

Katie sat down on the floor near the Christmas tree and soon all the kids were sitting near her in a circle. "But I didn't bring a present," said Brian.

"Oh, there are plenty of presents for everybody," said Lizzie slyly. "Sit by me, Adèle Hélene." She patted a place on the floor.

Adèle Hélene had been watching sulkily from across the room. Finally she shrugged her shoulders and joined the others. "Ah, I hope at least somebody thought to bring me a gift," she said.

"Don't worry," said Katie brightly. "I'm sure there's a very special one for you."

Lizzie had put on a Santa hat and was passing around the gifts she'd brought. Immediately, kids started tearing off the wrapping paper. There were small shrieks of delight as they discovered packs of gum and funny items from the dollar store.

"Here's one for you, Vanessa." Lizzie smiled as she handed her a tiny wrapped object.

"Ooh, I love presents! This party's looking up," said Vanessa, opening her package. "But what's this?" She turned over a small plastic figurine of a cow in her hands and then held it up for everyone to see.

"That's a *vache*, Vanessa," explained Lizzie. "That's what they call a cow in French. A *vache*. Although I think it's a pretty one and not a *vache laide*, don't you?"

Vanessa looked at the cow in her hands, all color vanishing from her face as she slowly figured out what Lizzie was saying. She looked at the little cow, she looked at Adèle Hélene, and she hurled it at her, spluttering, "Ugly cow? Ugly cow? If I'm an ugly cow, then you're a . . . a . . . I don't know what, but something bad, really bad. And ugly, too." In a fury, Vanessa started tearing up all the wrapping paper around her. Talia Fernandez tried to pat her on the back, but she shrugged her off. The rest of the kids, their presents opened and forgotten, had returned to the Twister game or were over at the refreshments table, where Mrs. Lexington was serving generous slices of cake with green and red frosting.

Meanwhile, Laurie was looking at a small, framed photo of a particularly scraggly mutt, which she had just opened. "I'm beginning to catch on. Is this a *chien*, Adèle Hélene? Is that what you call a dog in French? A *chien*?"

"Perhaps," muttered Adèle Hélene, pouting.

Lizzie was now standing in front of Adèle Hélene, holding out one last gift. "I didn't forget you!"

Adèle Hélene glared at her and grabbed the present. "And what have you given me? A goat or a goose, perhaps?" She forced herself to laugh — until she opened the present. It was a small tube of medicine. Adèle Hélene peered at it, reading the label carefully, and sounding out the words, "Anti-acne medication." She gave Lizzie a frightening smile. "How clever of you. I see you're learning French."

"I thought the real *bouton* needed the pimple cream. Not me." Lizzie tossed her head at Laurie and Vanessa. "C'mon, girls. My mom's waiting in the driveway. Party at my house." And all three girls grabbed their coats and flounced out.

Adèle Hélene glanced around her and sighed. "I am bored with this party and these childish games. If we were at Versailles, I would be chatting with the queen, and her son might even ask me to dance."

"You must really miss it," said Katie, glancing at her wristwatch. "C'mon upstairs to my room and I'll fix your hair for you. It's all falling out in the back."

Adèle Hélene narrowed her eyes suspiciously. "That is thoughtful of you, Katie. *Surprisingly* thoughtful."

"It's nothing, right? Just a *petit rien*."

"So you've been studying French, too?"

"A little bit of the language but more of the history. And I've got to tell you something." She lowered her voice to a whisper as the girls climbed the stairs. "I don't think you're going to have to marry that guy after all."

"What?" Adèle Hélene stopped. She was stunned.

"Nope. That's the good news. The bad news is everything's changed while you've been away. You ought to know that. A lot of people have left the country, the king and queen are in jail, and, frankly, it's not such a safe place for you aristocrats anymore." Katie took Adèle Hélene's arm and shut the door behind them, taking one last look at her watch.

"Here's the thing, Adèle Hélene. It's really not safe at Versailles anymore. As soon as you get there, you will have to go immediately to the main gate, where a blue carriage will be waiting for you. Get in it and don't open the door for anyone but Mr. Dee. Okay?"

"Why are you telling me all this? I'm staying here."

"Of course you are. But if for some reason you decide to go back later, please find the blue carriage. The blue carriage. I'm serious." Katie pulled a cloak from Adèle Hélene's trunk. "Could you put this on for a minute?" Katie draped the cloak around Adèle Hélene's shoulders, looked at her watch again, and bit her lip. Where were they?

"Why?" said Adèle Hélene. "What are you up to, Katie Lexington?"

Just then, Neil Carmody and Josh burst into the room.

"What's Neil doing here?" asked Katie, pretending to be surprised.

"I tried to stop him, but he said he just had to give her a present."

"Why can't he give me a present if he wants to?" demanded Adèle Hélene. "What do you have for me? Let me see."

Shyly, Neil Carmody held out a small box to Adèle Hélene.

Katie took another look at her watch and nodded at Josh.

"What's inside?" said Josh.

Adèle Hélene threw open the box, ripped apart the tissue paper, and pulled out a thin golden chain. Dangling from the end of it was the golden hourglass, with only two sparkling grains of sand left to fall. Adèle Hélene's eyes widened. Her mouth opened. But Katie and Josh would never know what she was going to say. The last grain of sand fell, there was a blinding flash of blue light and a noise like a sonic boom, and Adèle Hélene was gone. Completely gone.

Neil rubbed his eyes. "What happened?"

"What?" said Katie.

"What?" said Josh.

"But . . . but . . . where'd she go?" asked Neil, a wild look in his eyes. He opened up the closet door and then got on his knees and looked under the bed.

"What are you doing?" asked Katie.

"Adèle Hélene. One moment she was standing right there and the next . . . *Poof!* I mean . . . I mean . . . she vanished."

"Really?" said Katie.

"Really?" said Josh. "I thought she just walked out the door."

"Yeah," agreed Katie. "She just walked out the door. But thanks for giving her the necklace. I thought that would convince her to go home."

Neil still seemed completely dazed. Josh patted him on the back. "That girl made you crazy, Neil. C'mon, let's go have some cocoa."

And that was just what they did.

EPILOGUE: THANK YOU NOTES

On Christmas morning, Josh and Katie woke up at the crack of dawn. When they had finally managed to drag their parents downstairs, they started tearing open their presents. Mr. Lexington admired his latest tie from Katie. Mrs. Lexington was thrilled to have a gorgeous new scrapbook. Katie was surrounded by CDs, games, books, and the digital camera she'd always wanted. Josh was happy, too, with his new soccer ball, video games, and even the sensible sweater from a great-aunt he'd met only once before.

As their parents poured themselves another cup of coffee and Josh hooked up his new game to the television, Katie noticed something else under the tree. It was a wooden box tied with a lace ribbon.

"I don't remember seeing that before," said Mrs. Lexington. "Did you put that one under the tree, Abner?"

Mr. Lexington shook his head.

Katie noticed that the tree skirt around the box seemed to be singed, and the box felt strangely warm in her hands. There was a note on it.

"Hey, listen to this," she called to her family. "It's from Adèle Hélene." Everyone gathered around her as she read. " '*My dear family, as soon as we arrived safely in London, Le Comte du Dee urged me to send you all a small token of my appreciation. As I didn't think something from our finer shops would be suitable for you, I arranged for le comte to have this item delivered to your house.*'"

"How surprisingly thoughtful," said Mrs. Lexington. "I guess."

"Open it, open it," said Mr. Lexington eagerly.

Katie carefully untied the lace, lifted the lid of the box, and immediately started laughing.

"What is it?" said Josh.

"They're for you," said Katie. And she pulled out a pair of brand-new, top-of-the-line, twenty-first-century sneakers.

"I always said that girl had class," said Mr. Lexington.

"What's wrong with my sneakers?" cried Josh. But even he had to admit to himself that these new ones were *very* cool. In fact, he couldn't wait to try them on.

BACK WITH ADÈLE HÉLENE MARIE LOUISE MARGUERITE DE LA BOUCHE

France in 1789

You live in one of the most beautiful palaces in the world — Versailles. It has more than 1,000 rooms, which are filled with every imaginable luxury: paintings, tapestries, plush carpets, solid silver furniture, bejeweled candlesticks on marble stands, and walls of mirrors and gold. Fountains splash in the beautiful sculpture-filled gardens, and men and women, dressed in the finest satins and silks, laugh and jest while they wait for a glimpse of the king and queen. But you must also cover your nose with a perfume-scented handkerchief: More than 10,000 people — aristocrats, their many servants, and hangers-on — are crammed into tiny apartments without any bathrooms. Versailles, built on a swamp, literally stinks. Rats, attracted by the mountains of food left lying around, swarm underneath the velvet cushions of the furniture. Sometimes mice even nest in the elaborate flour-covered hairdos of the lovely ladies!

And there's not much to do. You spend a lot of time waiting around and gossiping with the other courtiers and talking about how bored you are. You while away the idle hours playing cards, making up nicknames for one another, attending musical performances, and worrying about what to wear next.

Still, it's an honor to even be at Versailles. To attend the king and queen, you must prove that your family is "born," that you can trace your nobility back to 1400 — at least. Unfortunately, being an aristocrat will cause you *a lot* of trouble in just a few years.

"This is some palace!"

Your Wealth

You always need more money — because you spend it like there's no tomorrow. (Actually, there isn't going to be a tomorrow, but you don't know that yet. . . .) You have a château, a house in Paris, an apartment at Versailles, and so many cooks, maids, gardeners, stable boys, tutors, and other servants that you can barely keep track of them. You have to entertain. Plus you have to wear the latest fashions — and the biggest jewels. Where do you get your money? You don't work, obviously. Most of it comes from your property — what the crops produce and what the peasants have to pay you for the use of your land. You get an income from your duties at court — handing the queen her nightgown, for instance. And, luckily, you don't have to pay taxes. Only the poor people have to do that. Still, there never seems to be enough, so you buy everything on "credit," which you conveniently never pay. And you gamble. And you play the king's lottery that *he* holds when he needs to raise a little more cash.

Fashion

As one of your court friends commented, "It's pointless being rich if no one knows." The best way to display your wealth and position is with your clothes. If you're a woman, you wear enormous dresses, stretched over six-foot-wide hoop skirts, that are covered in lace and ribbons and jewels. You wear elegant high heels, and your hair is curled and powdered, and decorated with feathers and ribbons and sculptures of ships and castles that can make it over three feet tall! No wonder the halls in the palaces are so large. They need to be so you can show off your outfits!

If you're a man, you wear brightly colored satin breeches and brocaded waistcoats and shirts no less elaborately decorated than the women's. You either powder your hair with flour paste or wear an elaborate wig. In Paris alone, there are more than 1,200 wigmakers with 6,000 assistants!

Marriage and Family

One of the best ways to get more money is to marry the right person. Marriage is mostly a business transaction and it is considered highly unusual, and even unfashionable, to actually love your wife or husband. Of course, you don't have to spend that much time together — and often lead completely separate lives, not even living in the same place.

Your parents may not be very close to you, either. Unless your mother, like the queen, is interested in some of the newfangled parenting ideas, she will give you to someone else to be nursed right after you are born and then turn you over to tutors or a convent school when you are six or seven. You may not see your parents very often at all. But they do get to decide who you marry — and if you don't obey them, they can ship you off to a convent and make you become a nun.

Education

Some of the greatest books, plays, and works of philosophy are being written in France right now — but you probably aren't reading them. You have learned

to curtsy and bow
properly, can do all
the latest dances,
ride to hunt, sing,
paint, and amuse
yourself, but you
may not have
spent a lot of time
cracking the books.
It's just not necessary
for your position in life. What you need to know are
the rules about how to behave at Court.

Food

What better way to while away the tedious hours
than to think about eating? For breakfast, you may have
coffee or a cup of hot chocolate, but by dinner, the main
meal, you will be ready for as many as twenty-nine
different courses — featuring such delicacies as filet of
venison with truffled partridge, capon stuffed with oys-
ters, endive with vinaigrette, boiled pigeons, artichokes,
duckling in orange sauce, custard tarts, whipped cream,
and all kinds of sweets. The king often makes himself ill
from eating too much pastry.

Not on the menu, however, is anything made with tomatoes or potatoes. These foods from America are known but used only experimentally or as decorations.

Everybody Else

Most people are *very* poor. Severe weather has meant many seasons of failed crops, and the price of bread is outrageous. There are often riots for food in Paris. The peasants are burdened by terrible taxes that they must pay to their wealthy landlords (you), and often they have nothing to eat but grass, boiled cabbage stalks, and bread made from ferns. There is plenty of food in France, but they can't afford it.

The bourgeoisie — shopkeepers, businessmen, and tradespeople — as well as some of the more educated aristocrats think it's time to change the government. They have had enough of the king's absolute power. Looking to their friends in America, who won their freedom from the British, they want to see a more democratic country — where everybody has a say about taxes, the use of the land, and the law.

Liberty, Equality, Fraternity!

These words thrill the hearts of the poor peasants but are not good news for you, an aristocrat. The party's over. At first, the leaders of the Revolution try to get the king to share his power with the people, but he is so obstinate about his position that eventually hundreds of angry peasants will storm Versailles and imprison him, the queen, and their children. Your family will probably lose their lands and houses, too; but if you are lucky, you will keep your head and escape to England or America or Italy. Many of your friends, however, will die by the newly invented guillotine in the coming chaos that sweeps the country. During the Reign of Terror, over 16,000 people will be beheaded.

A French–English Dictionary

allons-y — let's go

au revoir — good-bye

bouton — pimple (also a button)

c'est fantastique — that's fantastic

c'est horrible — that's horrible

c'est très belle — that's very pretty

charmant — charming

château — castle/palace

chien — dog

cochon — pig

corneille — crow

derrière — behind

grand — big

laide — ugly

merci — thank you

monsieur — Mr.

Noel — Christmas

non — no

oui — yes

petit — small

poulet — chicken

rien — nothing

s'il vous plaît — if you please

vache — cow

voilà — there you go

ABOUT THE AUTHOR

Perdita Finn's great-great grandmother was French. That's probably why she loves pastries so much. She currently lives in the Catskill Mountains with her husband, two children, four cats, and a dachshund who is eager to go to Paris as he has heard that dogs are allowed in restaurants there.